To my niece and nephew,

Maya and Milan

Homecoming

歸 來

Christian Beamish 著
吳泳霈 譯
朱正明 繪

Paulo was a young boy who lived on the island of Santiago in the Cape Verde Islands off the West Coast of Africa. Almost every day after school the boy stopped by an old lighthouse to visit his friend Joaquim, the old lighthouse keeper. The lighthouse tower stood tall and white at the top of the point over the sparkling blue sea. One lone palm tree swayed in the soft breeze and the sun shined down on the flat stones of the lighthouse courtyard.

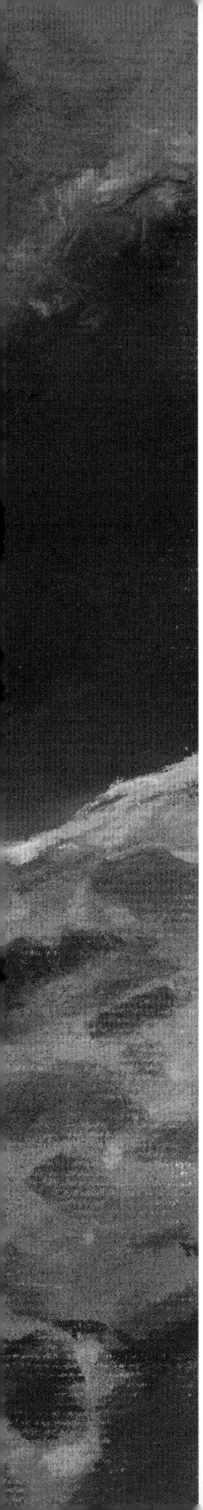

On this particular day, Paulo heard a guitar playing and a woman singing at the lighthouse. She had a beautiful voice. Paulo walked across the field with the crumbling stonewall, and as the boy got closer, he could hear the singing and the guitar more clearly.

Paulo stood at the rusted front gate of the lighthouse and peered into the courtyard. The old man Joaquim sat in a chair strumming a guitar and a large woman wearing a shimmering red dress stood singing under the shade canopy. Her voice seemed to float above the courtyard and drift out over the clear, tropical sea. She sang the words, "*How I loved you in my youth*."

The old man played the guitar with a faint smile and watched the woman as she sang. There was a glass pitcher of water, two plates, some cheese, olives, and a half-eaten loaf of bread on the table—the remnants of their lunch. When the song ended the woman laughed and sat down, she reached over and squeezed Joaquim's arm. "I am so glad to be here!" she said.

"It has been too long, Claudia," Joaquim replied. The old man leaned his guitar against the table and poured the woman a glass of water.

They still had not seen Paulo who was standing at the front gate. The boy turned and started walking away, but Joaquim spotted him and called out, “Paulo! I was hoping you would come by today!”

The large woman in the shimmering red dress smiled. Her teeth were very white and her dark hair was tied back with a ribbon; her skin was the color of coffee with a little cream stirred in.

“Come in, Paulo!” the old man said as he walked across the courtyard to open the front gate for the boy. “My granddaughter has come to visit me!”

The woman stood up and kissed Paulo on both cheeks in the custom of the Cape Verde islands. “So this is Paulo!” she said, holding the boy by his shoulders. “I am Claudia. Grandfather has told me so much about you!”

Paulo looked down at his sandals. “Your singing is very pretty,” the boy said quietly.

Claudia’s eyes lit up like Joaquim’s did when he smiled or laughed, and she said, “Thank you, Paulo!” and hugged the boy as he stood stiffly with his arms at his sides.

"I told Claudia about the first time you came to the lighthouse, Paulo," Joaquim said smiling as he slapped the boy lightly on the arm. "Remember?" the old man asked, "I thought you were spying on me!"

"I remember," Paulo said with an embarrassed smile. He sat down on the bench that the old man had made from the top rail of a wrecked fishing boat. "You never told me that you played the guitar, Joaquim," Paulo said.

The old man picked up the guitar and laid it in his lap. “That is because I only play with Claudia,” he said.

“Grandfather!” Claudia said emphatically, leaning forward with her hand on the old man’s knee. “You must play!”

“Not alone, my dear,” Joaquim said patting his granddaughter’s hand.

“You see, Paulo,” Claudia said to the boy, “we left the island during the drought. Mother and I emigrated to Europe.”

Joaquim looked out to sea. The old man rubbed the whiskers on his chin. He seemed to be thinking about something, or remembering perhaps.

"But you stayed, Joaquim?" Paulo asked.

The lighthouse keeper looked at his granddaughter and then turned to Paulo. His eyes were welled with tears. "I am the lighthouse keeper," Joaquim said.

"Grandfather taught me to sing when I was a little girl," Claudia said to Paulo.

The old man smiled. "What a beautiful voice!" he said. "From the beginning," Joaquim recalled, "her voice soared like a bird flying over the sea. Now she sings concerts in Europe." Joaquim smiled proudly.

"When I sing," Claudia said, "part of me comes back here, to this lighthouse. I feel it like the sunshine on my shoulders. I come home when I sing."

“So you are not so far apart after all,” Paulo observed.

“No, I suppose we are not so far apart in that way,” Joaquim agreed.

“And if you play your guitar, Grandfather,” Claudia said, “we will be together in the music.”

“Well, we are together right now!” Joaquim exclaimed. “Why don’t we play another song?”

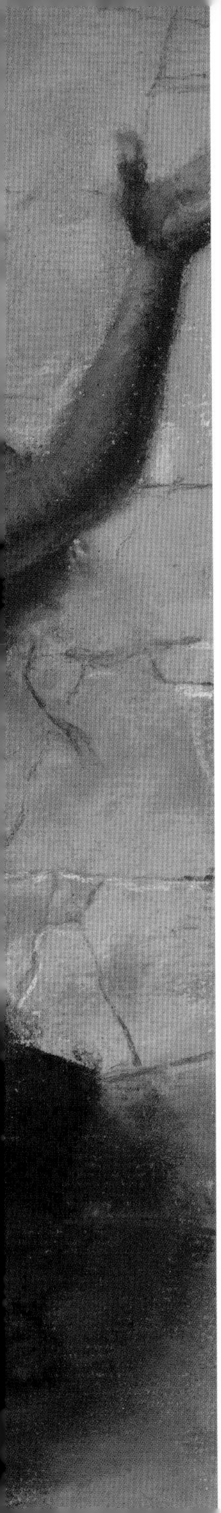

The old man picked up his guitar and played a flourishing scale. Claudia stood up again and lifted her arms. Her voice climbed and dipped with the rhythm of Joaquim's guitar. Paulo closed his eyes and tilted his face up to the warm sun. It was a sad but beautiful song.

Paulo stood up while Claudia was singing and made a slight bow to her. The boy turned and nodded to Joaquim, and then pushed open the rusted front gate. As Paulo walked across the field toward his house, he looked back at the lighthouse once more.

It seemed entirely possible to him that such soft and beautiful music might soar all the way to Europe, or even from Europe back to Cape Verde.

Vocabulary

P.2

lone [lon] adj. 孤獨的

sway [swe] v. 搖擺

courtyard [ˋkort͵jɑrd] n. 庭院

P.5

crumble [ˋkrʌmbl̩] v. 碎裂

P.7

rusted [ˋrʌstɪd] adj. 生鏽的

strum [strʌm] v. 彈 (吉他等的弦樂器)

shimmer [ˋʃɪmɚ] v. 發微光；閃爍

canopy [ˋkænəpi] n. 遮雨篷

P.9

pitcher [ˋpɪtʃɚ] n. 大水罐；水壺

olive [`ɑlɪv] n. 橄欖

remnant [`rɛmnənt] n. 剩餘

P.11

spot [spɑt] v. 認出；發現

P.14

sandal [`sændḷ] n. 涼鞋

P.16

slap [slæp] v. 用手掌打

rail [rel] n. 圍欄

P.18

emphatically [ɪm`fætɪkḷɪ] adv. 強調的

drought [draʊt] n. 乾旱；旱災

emigrate [`ɛmə,gret] v. 移居外國

P.20

whisker [`hwɪskɚ] n. 鬢鬚 (常用複數)

P.23

soar [sor] v. 往上飛舞；高飛

P.24

exclaim [ɪk`sklem] v. 呼喊；大聲說出

P.27

flourish [`flɝɪʃ] v. 繁茂

scale [skel] n. 音階

tilt [tɪlt] v. 使傾斜

故事中譯

P.2

保羅是一個住在西非外海維德角群島中聖地牙哥島的小男孩。幾乎每天放學後，這個男孩都會順道去燈塔拜訪他的朋友喬昆——一位年老的燈塔看守人。這座白色的燈塔高高矗立在海岬的尖端，俯視著這片閃閃發光的藍色海洋。唯一的一棵棕櫚樹在微風中搖曳著，而陽光照耀著燈塔庭院中的石板路。

P.5

在這個特別的日子，保羅聽到燈塔處傳來吉他彈奏和女人唱歌的聲音；她有一副美妙的嗓子。保羅穿過那片有碎石牆的空地；當他愈靠近燈塔，他愈能清楚聽到歌聲和吉他聲。

P.7

保羅站在燈塔生鏽的前門外，往庭院裡面瞧。老人喬昆坐在椅子上彈著吉他，而一位高大、豐腴，穿著閃亮紅洋裝的女人，正站在遮陽篷下唱歌。她的歌聲似乎飄上庭院上方，傳向清澈的熱帶海洋。她唱著：「*當我年少時，我是多麼愛你！*」

P.9

老人彈著吉他，臉上帶著淡淡的笑意，注視著那個女人唱歌。桌子上放著裝水的玻璃壺、兩個盤子、一些起司和橄欖，還有一條吃了一半的麵包——他們吃剩的午餐。歌曲結束後，女人笑了，她坐下來伸出手握了握喬昆的手臂，說：「我真高興能回到這裡！」

喬昆回答：「克勞蒂亞，妳真的太久沒回來了。」老人將吉他斜靠在桌邊，然後倒了一杯水給那個女人。

P.11

他們仍然沒有看到站在前門的保羅。當男孩轉身正準備離開時，喬昆發現了他，對他喊：「保羅，我正希望你今天會順道過來呢！」

那位身穿閃亮紅洋裝的高大女人微笑著。她的牙齒非常潔白，深色的頭髮用緞帶綁在腦後，皮膚像是咖啡拌進些許奶油的顏色。

P.13

老人一邊走過庭院為男孩打開前門，一邊說：「進來吧，保羅！我的孫女來看我了！」

女人站了起來，依維德角的習俗親了親保羅的雙頰。她搭著男孩的肩膀說：「原來你就是保羅！我是克勞蒂亞。爺爺已經跟我說了許多關於你的事呢！」

P.14

保羅低頭盯著他的涼鞋，小聲的說：「妳的歌聲很美。」

克勞蒂亞的眼睛亮了起來，像喬昆微笑或大笑時一樣。她說：「保羅，謝謝你！」並擁抱他；保羅僵硬的站著，雙臂緊貼在身體兩側。

P.16

喬昆輕輕拍了拍男孩的手臂，笑著說：「保羅，我跟

克勞蒂亞說了你第一次來燈塔的情形。」他接著問：「還記得嗎？我當時還以為你在偷窺我呢！」

保羅帶著難為情的笑容說：「我記得。」他在那張老人用破損漁船的船圍做成的長板凳上坐了下來。保羅又說：「喬昆，你從來沒告訴過我你會彈吉他。」

P.18

老人拿起吉他放在大腿上，說：「那是因為我只幫克勞蒂亞伴奏。」

克勞蒂亞傾身向前，將手放在老人的膝蓋上，堅決的說：「爺爺！您一定要彈！」

喬昆拍拍他孫女的手說：「親愛的，我不要獨奏。」

克勞蒂亞對男孩說：「保羅，你知道嗎？我們在鬧乾旱時離開了這座島；我和媽媽移民到歐洲去了。」

P.20

喬昆望向大海，搓揉著下巴上的鬍鬚。他似乎是在思考，又或許，是在回憶往事。

保羅問：「喬昆，但是你卻留了下來？」

燈塔看守人看一看他的孫女，然後轉向保羅；他的眼睛湧出淚水。他說：「我是這座燈塔的看守人啊！」

P.23

克勞蒂亞對保羅說：「當我還是小女孩時，是爺爺教我唱歌的。」

老人微笑著說：「多麼美妙的歌聲啊！」他回憶著：「從一開始，她的歌聲就像鳥兒翱翔在海面上一樣。現在，她在歐洲的音樂會裡演唱呢。」喬昆驕傲的微笑著。

克勞蒂亞說：「當我唱歌的時候，一部分的我會回到這裡，回到這座燈塔，好像陽光正照耀在我的肩膀上。當我唱歌的時候，我就感覺彷彿回到家鄉一般。」

P.24

保羅說出他的想法：「那麼其實你們沒有離得很遠啊。」

喬昆贊同：「嗯，我想這樣看來，我們並不是離得很遠。」

克勞蒂亞說：「而且爺爺，如果您彈奏吉他的話，我們就能在音樂中相聚了。」

喬昆激動的說：「是啊！我們現在就聚在一起呀！我們何不再合奏一曲呢？」

P.27

老人拿起他的吉他，彈奏出流暢的旋律。克勞蒂亞再次站了起來，並舉起她的雙臂；她的歌聲隨著喬昆吉他的旋律高低起伏。保羅閉上雙眼，將臉微微仰向溫暖的太陽。那是一首悲傷而優美的歌曲。

P.29

當克勞蒂亞還在唱著歌時，保羅站了起來，向她微微一鞠躬，又轉身向喬昆點點頭，然後推開生鏽的前門。保羅穿過空地要回家時，他再次回頭看看燈塔。

P.30

對保羅來說，這樣柔和美妙的樂聲，似乎真能一路翱翔到歐洲，或是從歐洲飄洋過海傳回維德角。

Exercises

Part One. Reading Comprehension

Answer the following questions about the story in short sentences.

1. What did Paulo hear when he went to the lighthouse at the beginning of the story?
2. Who was the woman in red dress?
3. Why had Joaquim never told Paulo that he could play a guitar?
4. What had happened to Joaquim and Claudia during the drought?

Part Two. Topics for Discussion

Answer the following questions in your own words and try to support your answers with details in the story. There are no correct answers to the questions in this section.

1. What kind of personality do you think Claudia has?
2. Why do you think Joaquim had never played guitar without Claudia?
3. Claudia said in the story, "*When I sing, part of me comes back here, to this lighthouse. I feel it like the sunshine on my shoulders. I come home when I sing.*" What did she mean? Explain.

Answers

Part One. Reading Comprehension

1. A guitar playing and a woman singing.
2. Joaquim's granddaughter.
3. That was because he only played with Claudia.
4. Claudia and her mother left the island and emigrated to Europe. But Joaquim stayed.

旅遊導覽

維德角的音樂風情

非洲的音樂在世界民族音樂中，一直佔有一席之地。這塊遼闊的大陸擁有眾多的種族和複雜的殖民歷史，因此，異國文化在這塊土地上，譜出了許多精彩的音樂。

位於西非外海的維德角共和國也是一個歷史背景複雜的國家。它曾經是葡萄牙的殖民地，只是，在葡萄牙的殖民期間，並未替維德角帶來任何建設，貧困的生活迫使居民紛紛移居到美國、葡萄牙與法國等地，僅剩近三分之一的人口留在島上。不過，雖然生活窮困，維德角的人們仍然創造出了優美的音樂。

過去為殖民地的維德角，音樂風格相當多樣化，其中最富盛名的，是一種名為「Morna」的曲風。由於當地人生活窮困，時常用音樂抒發情感，Morna 就以感傷的曲調為主；每一首歌曲都是獨立的詩篇，內容訴說著愛與渴望，或生活的苦悶和憂鬱。也因此，Morna 音樂常被比喻為西非的「藍調」（藍調的起源為早期黑奴用來抒發鬱悶情緒的音樂)。演唱 Morna 音樂最有名的歌手為世界知名的西莎莉・亞艾芙拉 (Cesaria Evora)，她有「赤足歌后」之稱——這個稱號的由來，是因為她每次上台演唱時都赤著腳，以表達她對貧窮婦女及兒童的關懷。

關於樂器

Morna 音樂使用的樂器，較常見的有單簧管、手風琴、小提琴、吉他，和一種名為「葡萄牙四絃琴」(cavaquinho) 的當地樂器。

除了較抒情的 Morna 音樂之外，維德角還有其他各式各樣的樂風，顯示出這塊土地文化上的多元性。所以當你在欣賞來自維德角的音樂時，可能會發現有些曲子聽起來有爵士樂的味道，或是像巴西森巴舞曲熱情的曲調，這就是文化融合在音樂上的成果。

About the Author

Born March 15th, 1969 in Laguna Beach, Christian Beamish has always been attracted to the water. His father introduced him to the ocean at a very young age and he has been surfing for more than 25 years. In 1987, after graduating high school, Christian joined the U.S. Navy and worked in a construction battalion on many overseas projects. His Navy travels have been a very important part of his development as a writer since he was exposed to many interesting places and people. The time he spent in Cape Verde with the Navy was the basis for the Paulo and Joaquim stories: the unique culture of the islands and the way the people there are so closely connected to the sea. Christian currently lives in San Clemente, California and has plans to build an 18-foot sailboat for the next stage of his ocean development.

Author's Note: About *Homecoming*

I wanted to see a little bit more of old Joaquim's life. I imagined he had some kind of family (everyone comes from somewhere) and his granddaughter visiting was the image that came to me. The Cape Verde islands have a wonderful musical tradition with many fine singers and musicians and I wanted to show some of that in my story.

The Cape Verde islands have also been a very difficult place to live at times. There was a drought in the 1970s and many people left the islands. Today many Cape Verdians live overseas—especially in Portugal and in the northeastern United States—and I wanted Joaquim's daughter to represent the people who have left the islands and sometimes have a difficult time coming back to visit. The visit I wrote about in this story is important for Paulo because he learns more about his friend Joaquim.

關於繪者

朱正明

1959 年次，現居台北市。

年幼好塗鴉；自高中時期即選讀美工科，業畢次年 (1979) 考取國立藝術專科學校美術科西畫組，1982 年以西畫水彩類第一名畢業。

求學時期除水彩、素描技法之外，並對漫畫、卡通之藝術表現形式頗有興趣，役畢後工作項度側重於卡通、漫畫、插畫。

1999 年驟生再學之念，並於次年考取國立師範大學美術研究所西畫創作組；2003 年取得美術碩士學位，該年申請入師大附中實習教師獲准，次年 2004 年取得教育部頒發之美術科正式教師資格證書，目前仍為自由工作者身分。

國家圖書館出版品預行編目資料

Homecoming:歸來 / Christian Beamish著;朱正明繪;
吳泳霈譯.——初版一刷.——臺北市:三民,2005
面; 公分.——(愛閱雙語叢書.祕密基地系列④)
ISBN 957-14-4329-8 (精裝)

1. 英國語言—讀本

524.38 94012749

網路書店位址 http://www.sanmin.com.tw

© Homecoming
——歸來

著作人 Christian Beamish
繪　者 朱正明
譯　者 吳泳霈
發行人 劉振強
著作財產權人 三民書局股份有限公司
臺北市復興北路386號
發行所 三民書局股份有限公司
地址 / 臺北市復興北路386號
電話 / (02)25006600
郵撥 / 0009998-5
印刷所 三民書局股份有限公司
門市部 復北店 / 臺北市復興北路386號
重南店 / 臺北市重慶南路一段61號
初版一刷 2005年8月
編　號 S 805691
定　價 新臺幣貳佰元整
行政院新聞局登記證局版臺業字第〇二〇〇號

ISBN 957-14-4329-8 (精裝)